Lailah's Lunchbox

A Ramadan Story

Reem Faruqi   Illustrations by Lea Lyon

"We won't be needing this for a while," said Lailah's mother, hanging up Lailah's lunchbox.

"Imagine! I won't be eating lunch for a month!" replied Lailah with a twirl.

"I won't have to pack lunch for a month!" said her mom with a bigger twirl.

*T*he year before, Lailah had wanted to fast with her best friends Hend and Ishrat during Ramadan, but Lailah's mom had insisted she was too small.

Remembering that, Lailah stopped twirling.

She missed her friends.

Moving from one continent to another had been hard.

Peachtree City

On the map in her atlas, North America and the Middle East were ten inches apart, but in real life she was so much farther away. She wished she was only ten inches away from Hend and Ishrat! She knew the sign by the highway said, "Peachtree City: You'll Love to Call It Home!" but she didn't agree with the sign. Abu Dhabi still felt like her home.

The next morning before sunrise, Lailah's mom gently nudged her. "Lailah," she whispered, "Sehri time!"

Lailah chomped on her chocolate chip pancakes with her eyes closed. "Delicious!" she said.

"Come! Let's pray now," said her mom.

After Sehri, Lailah snuggled back into her bed until her mom woke her up again, this time for school. As she left the house, her mom handed her a note. "Lailah, please give this note to Mrs. Penworth."

Without her lunchbox to carry, her fingers felt extra free and swingy.

She felt so light she skipped to the school bus stop!

O n the school bus, she read her mom's note:

Dear Mrs. Penworth,

This will be Lailah's first time fasting for the month of Ramadan so it is an exciting time for us.

Please excuse Lailah from lunch for this special month.

Thanks!
Mrs. Malik

Lailah didn't feel so bouncy anymore. What if Mrs. Penworth didn't know about Ramadan? No one else would be fasting with her. She folded the note into a teeny tiny square and hid it in her book bag.

*L*ailah walked slowly to her class. Her throat felt dry all morning. When lunchtime arrived, she still hadn't given Mrs. Penworth her note.

"Lailah, did you forget your lunch?" asked Mrs. Penworth.

Lailah opened her mouth to speak, but no words came out.

Samantha volunteered, "I'll share my lunch with Lailah!"

Mrs. Penworth shook her head. "Thank you for the offer, Samantha, but Lailah, please get a sandwich from the cafeteria."

Lailah followed her classmates to the cafeteria. "Lailah, do you want some of my cream roll?" asked Anna.

Lailah thought of telling Anna that she was fasting, but she didn't think anyone at Sunnyvale Elementary School knew about Ramadan. "No, thanks," she started to say. "I didn't bring my . . . ."

"Are you sure?" asked Anna, unwrapping the cream rolls.

Lailah watched the cream roll get smaller and smaller, and she didn't feel so sure. Cream rolls were her favorite.

She looked away. Her nose still smelled food.

Lailah wished she had given Mrs. Penworth the note. Even Isaiah's baloney sandwich looked tasty, and Lailah didn't even like baloney. Her stomach rumbled.

Suddenly, she had an idea. While everyone was busy eating, she sneaked out of the cafeteria. Her stomach stopped growling.

"Why, Lailah! It's a pleasure to see you, but what brings you here at lunchtime?" asked Mrs. Carman, the librarian.

Lailah felt safe among all the books. She opened her mouth, and this time her words tumbled out. Lailah told Mrs. Carman that Mrs. Penworth and her classmates didn't know she was fasting. She told her how she missed Hend and Ishrat. It felt good to tell someone all the words that had been inside her mind all morning, and especially to tell her about Ramadan.

Mrs. Carman understood. "You must feel special to fast this Ramadan," said the librarian with a smile.

"*I* do," said Lailah. "But why is it so hard to explain?"

"You know what I always do when I can't get my thoughts out, or when I get shy about talking?" asked Mrs. Carman. "I write my thoughts down."

ailah got to work. She wrote neatly, adding extra loops to her capital L. She worked so hard her cheeks turned pink.

Dear Mrs. Penworth,
 I didn't forget my lunchbox today. It's Ramadan. My mom finally let me fast. This means I won't be eating lunch for a month.
Sincerely,

Lailah

p.s. I'm Muslim!
p.p.s My mom wrote you a note too! Here it is!!
p.p.p.s. Here's a poem I wrote about Ramadan:

Ramadan is a month Muslims celebrate.
A time to count our blessings and appreciate.
Muslims fast before sunrise to sunset
But wait, that's not all just yet!

Ramadan is a time for lots of prayer.
We help the poor people to show we care!
So in the day I won't be eating any food
But hopefully will stay in a good mood!

Lailah hurried back to the cafeteria to join her class. Before school was out, she quietly dropped both notes onto Mrs. Penworth's desk.

The next morning Lailah swung her fingers as she waited for the school bus. Would Mrs. Penworth like her poem? Lailah hoped Mrs. Penworth wouldn't think she had forgotten her lunchbox again. She slowly climbed each step on the school bus.

In class, Mrs. Penworth didn't say anything, so Lailah wondered what had happened. At times like this, she wished Hend and Ishrat were there with her. They would know what to say!

At lunchtime Lailah's feet felt heavy. She was sure Mrs. Penworth hadn't seen the notes. Everyone would think she had forgotten her lunchbox again. As she was leaving class, Mrs. Penworth patted Lailah on the back and handed her a message. Mrs. Penworth had made her capital L in Lailah's name extra loopy!

Dear Lailah,

I enjoyed your lovely poem about Ramadan.
I'm impressed you're fasting. What a special time
for you! You and your family must be thrilled!

Would you share your poem with the class today
after lunch? You could go the library this month
instead of the cafeteria. Mrs. Carman is excited
to see you.

Sincerely,
Mrs. Penworth

p.s. Mrs. Carman told me you missed your friends.
I hope you keep making new friends with our class.

*L*ailah twirled all the way to the
library. She couldn't wait to share
her Ramadan poem with her class.

Later, at Iftar, she would
celebrate this day!

Author's Note

As a child, I remember growing up in Abu Dhabi wishing I could fast with my best friends Hend and Ishrat, but my mother thought I was too small to fast. When I finally was allowed to fast, I missed their company! Like Lailah, my family moved to Peachtree City, Georgia, all the way from Abu Dhabi, the capital of the United Arab Emirates.

During Ramadan, I found it challenging to explain to my non-Muslim friends why I was not eating lunch with them. The library became my safe place away from all the fragrant food smells, and I spent many hours there enjoying good books. I hope we all have the courage, like Lailah, to explain and celebrate our beliefs.

Contrary to what some may think, Ramadan is not all about food. It's about growing up and finally being able to fast.

It's about cherishing the family with whom you sit down every evening at sunset to open your fast. It's about praying with the community and sharing with those in need. It's about inviting friends over for Iftar and sending food to your neighbors. Lailah's poem is adapted from a note we used to stick on food my mother would send to our neighbors during Ramadan. It's a special month to celebrate and each year I look forward to it, with or without cream rolls!

Ramadan Mubarak!
(Have a blessed Ramadan!)

Glossary

Sehri: (In Arabic, *Suhoor*) a meal Muslims eat before sunrise during Ramadan to start their daily fast

Iftar: a meal Muslims eat at sunset during Ramadan to open the day's fast

Tilbury House Publishers

12 Starr Street

Thomaston, Maine 04861

800-582-1899

www.tilburyhouse.com

First hardcover edition: June 2015 • 10 9 8 7 6 5 4 3 2 1
ISBN 978-0-88448-431-8

DEDICATIONS

To Khalajee—without your support, this book would not be here!
Love and Duas to all my family including Nana, Daado, Amma, Abba,
Naoman, Zineera, Anisa, Tooba, and my sisters, Amena and Asna. —RF

For Eshal, my "Lailah," and Mrs. O'Donoghue's fifth-grade class
at Live Oak School in San Ramon, California. —LL

Library of Congress Cataloging-in-Publication Data

Faruqi, Reem, author.
Lailah's lunchbox / by Reem Faruqi; illustrated by Lea Lyon.
    pages cm
Summary: Lailah is delighted that she can fast during the month of Ramadan like her family and her friends
in Abu Dhabi, but finding a way to explain to her teacher and classmates in Atlanta is a challenge until she
gets some good advice from the librarian, Mrs. Carman.

ISBN 978-0-88448-431-8 (hardcover)
ISBN 978-0-88448-432-5 (ebook)
[1. Ramadan--Fiction. 2. Fasts and feasts--Islam--Fiction. 3. Muslims--Fiction. 4. Islam--Customs and
practices--Fiction. 5. Schools--Fiction. 6. Middle Eastern Americans--Fiction. 7. Moving, Household--
Fiction.] I. Lyon, Lea, 1945- illustrator. II. Title.
PZ7.1.F37Lai 2015
[Fic]--dc23
                    2014042485

Printed by Worzalla, Stevens Point, Wisconsin

M